LUDWIG BEMELMANS

SUNSHINE

A NOTE TO THE READER

As this book was first published in 1950, some of the
language might seem unfamiliar. Below are explanations
of some of the words and phrases that might be confusing.
These are marked with *.

Page 8
"perambulator"–a fancy word for "stroller" or "pram."

Page 9
"Mayflower descendant"–Mr. Sunshine, and others, thought
that the longer your family had been in the U.S., the more
well-behaved you'd be.

Page 13
"WILLIAM TELL"–The *William Tell Overture* by
Gioachino Rossini is a VERY LOUD piece of music.

Page 20
"good deportment"–This means "good behavior."
Not something Mr. Sunshine is demonstrating...

Page 41
"Central Park's Mall"–A walkway through the middle
of Central Park, from 66th to 72nd Street.

This edition first published in the United Kingdom in 2020 by
Thames & Hudson Ltd, 181A High Holborn, London WC1V 7QX

First published in the United States by Simon & Schuster, USA, in 1950
featuring portions from *Good Housekeeping* magazine published by
Hearst Magazines, Inc. in 1949.

This edition first published in 2020 in the United States of America by
Thames & Hudson Inc., 500 Fifth Avenue, New York, New York 10110

British Library Cataloguing-in-Publication Data
A catalogue record for this book is available from the British Library

Library of Congress Control Number 2019957046

ISBN 978-0-500-65235-0

Printed and bound in China by C&C Offset Printing Co. Ltd

Be the first to know about our new releases,
exclusive content and author events by visiting
thamesandhudson.com
thamesandhudsonusa.com
thamesandhudson.com.au

The boy has a poodle, the girl a setter,
And Mr. Sunshine is mailing a letter.
The letter contains the text of an ad
Saying an apartment is to be had.

TWO CHEERFUL ROOMS with bath in a building that truly hath atmosphere and old-world charm: in summer cool, in winter warm, venetian blinds, open fireplace, cross-ventilation, ample closet space, refrigerator and hardwood floor. A lovely view. Bus stops at door.

But the ceiling sagged and the hall was dark
At two hundred and three Gramercy Park.
Mr. Sunshine hung up a sign and fell
Asleep until someone rang his bell.

7

He got up from his soft seat
And rushed out into the street.
"Go," he said with angry face.
"Go, look for some other place!

"I don't permit cats or doggies,
People who have noisy hobbies,
People with perambulators,*
People who keep alligators,

"Artists, acrobats or players,
Traveling salesmen or soothsayers.
To all those and sundry I say
Thank you kindly, go away!"

And so for evident reasons
For several long seasons,
The apartment at two hundred and three
Was free of any tenantry.

8

At last a feeble lady's voice
Inquired whether there was any noise
Or commotion in the neighborhood,
And when he said "No," she said "Very good."
And that she'd be there to see
The charming apartment at half-past three.

As Sunshine stood watching the clock
A sweet old lady came down the block.
"Punctual," he said, "right on the dot.
In a tenant that means an awful lot!

"Bless me," said Sunshine, "here advances
A lady in comfortable circumstances.
An unattached female that pays the rent
Year in, year out, to the last cent.
Here comes indeed the perfect tenant–
Perhaps a Mayflower descendant."*

In front of the house she stopped and bent low.
With a small whiskbroom she cleared the snow.
And then she fed the pigeons and starlings
And all her other feathered darlings.

Quietly as a mouse,
She came into the house.
"Oh," she said, "it's a perfect delight,
It's awfully homey, it's just right.

"It's exactly the kind
Of a place I hoped to find."
"You may have a five-year lease."
"I'm ready to sign it, if you please."

"And here is a check
For the first month's rent."
"Dear Madam," said Sunshine,
"You're heaven-sent."

He did not know—
the poor fool—

That Miss Moore was running a music school.

And here we see how Sunshine likes
To be awakened by the Stars and Stripes.
He dressed in haste and almost fell
Downstairs to the strains of…

… WILLIAM TELL.*

Miss Moore was totally immersed
In music whenever she rehearsed.
"I advise you," said Sunshine, "to desist and cease,
Or I shall be forced to cancel your lease."

She simply said: "Children—give it all you've got!"
"I'm a patient man—I stand for a lot!
But Madam," he said, "this is the last straw.
I shall see you in a court of law!"

And after making all that fuss
He ran to catch a Fifth Avenue bus.

He rushed to his lawyer and said: "George, will you please,
Thoroughly examine this lease.
And tell me how I can best
Rid myself of this awful pest."

The lawyer took his time and then he said:
"Sunshine, I'm very much afraid
This is a perfectly good lease.
Music docs not disturb the peace.

"This is an unhappy hour.
You underestimated the power
Of a woman,
Whom no Judge would dare to summon.

"My advice is: in your place
I would make up my mind to face
The music, and if things don't improve
I counsel you to pack and move."

Sunshine tried hard for a while
To find another domicile.
And he discovered that it was true
That rents were high and places few.

Here we behold the mean old grouch
Trying to sleep on his office couch.

Miss Moore felt fine in the early hours
Although the radio prophesied showers.
She exclaimed: "Upon my soul
I've never owned a parasol!"

She finished her crumpet and then she drank
A second cup of tea and went to the bank.
She drew enough money for the rent
And an additional sum to be spent
For a varied assortment
Of prizes for good deportment.*

The sky turned suddenly gray
As Miss Moore was on her way,
And the rain began to fall
As she came to an auctioneer's hall.

Inside the hall a fellow
Held up an antique umbrella.
And the voice of the auctioneer
Bellowed: "Please let me hear
If any of you ladies and gents
Will offer me ten cents."

Miss Moore raised her right hand
And the man on the auction stand
Shouted: "Going, going, gone,
Sold to the lady that stands there alone."

Miss Moore paid
And said,

"Thank you so much.
 I had no idea that such
 Bargains were still to be had.
 I'll be more than glad
 To send a lot more
 People to your lovely store.
 And now I'll bid you good day."

But he said: "There's a balance you have to pay."

"Young man, explain that to me please."

"They're two thousand umbrellas, at ten cents apiece.

They've been lost or found and have gone astray

On the trains and stations of Manhattan's subway."

"Oh, dear," said Miss Moore. "This just about

Leaves me flat–it cleans me out."

"I'm sorry, dear lady. All I can say

Is, you bid for the lot and you have to pay."

And so that afternoon came a truck
And everyone on the block
Said, "Poor
Miss Moore."

And the neighborhood gossip, a woman named Hattie,
Observed: "The old girl must have gone batty."

Miss Moore was totally immersed
In umbrellas and music as she rehearsed.

Sunshine said: "I'm glad at last to see
You up a proverbial tree.
I'm happy, Miss Moore, to let you know
That the game is up and out you go.

"You came here under false pretenses—
I must have been out of my senses.
This will teach me a lesson I'll not forget.
Pack up now, for this place is to let.

"Get out with your doggies and with your cats,
Go rid my house of these noisy brats."
Miss Moore just tapped with her baton
And said, "In a moment, children, we'll go on.
My little friends, I'm very sorry.

"Please, don't any of you worry.
We shall simply wait for rain
And sell the old umbrellas again.
We shall continue to occupy this place;
The law gives us a few days' grace.

"With the Lord's help, we'll soon send
Mr. Sunshine his overdue rent.
Sunshine, Sunshine, go away
And come again some other day!"

In answer to the powerful prayers
Of the children, who refused to stop,

The sun was blotted out by layers
Of clouds, and the sky gave up.

Drainpipes gurgled, gutters choked,
And the citizenry was soaked.

The children left the house as the rain
Came down like out of a water main.

The rain did not take pity
On the Mayor's reception committee.

This customer is a United Nations delegate;
The tall building is called the Empire State.

It was windy, cold, and showery,
And tough work down on the Bowery.

Miss Moore ascended to Columbia Heights
And sold umbrellas to Brooklynites.

The last umbrella was sold in Astoria

To a visitor who flew in from Peoria.

After the downpour, Miss Moore
Suddenly was no longer poor.
There was no more worry about the rent,
And each child got a new instrument.

They played in Central Park's Mall*
And gave a concert in Carnegie Hall.

And as the tree was lit up in the dark,
They celebrated Christmas in Gramercy Park.

O Holy Night

Late that night a man came to the house.
He muttered that he wasn't Santa Claus.

"You'll never guess," he said, "who this is!
  I just came to wish you a Merry Christmas.
  And to tell you that I feel like a heel—
  For months I haven't enjoyed a meal.
  And the thing that mostly grates me—
  Is that my own lawyer hates me.

"But" pleaded Sunshine, "if I only could
  Come back to this lovely neighborhood—
  I like doggies, birds, and cats;
  Oh, I'll even put up with rats.
  I've become immune to noises,
  I love little children's voices,
  And I certainly make no exceptions
  To concerts and musical selections."

And so Miss Moore smiled quietly and told
  Mr. Sunshine to come in out of the cold.
  He thanked her as he knocked the sleet
  And snow from his frozen feet.
  The cat sat on his lap and purred with mirth,
  The dog lay at his feet, and peace was on earth.

AFTERWORD

Sunshine is my favorite of all my father's children's books. The story begins and ends at Gramercy Park, which is the New York area where I spent my childhood. Gramercy Park is the sole private park in Manhattan. It is open to the public only on Christmas Eve. The doorman at the now defunct Hotel Irving, our home for five or so years, would walk me to the closest park gate, unlock it with his key, and then close and relock the gate once I was inside. The Hotel Irving is just out of sight of the picture on page 10.

The character of Mr. Sunshine was, I'm certain, inspired by a landlord who, during a dire housing crisis, refused to renew the lease on our apartment. The landlord occupied the first four floors of 20 Gramercy Park. We had most of the fifth (top) floor. He had decided to kick us out so he could convert our apartment into a movie screening room for his guests.

The house where Miss Moore conducts her music school reminds me of the building where I briefly took violin classes.

Bozy, my father's dog, a Bouvier des Flandres, appears in three of the book's pictures, as does Kitty de Belvedere, my Yorkshire Terrier and tenth birthday present. The picture and rhyme on page 5 always make me smile. Before my parents' marriage, my father had a setter. When I was four, we got a Poodle puppy we named Toots. She and my mother immediately bonded and there was no question that sweet Toots was my mother's dog.

My father wrote the first lines of *Madeline* on the back of a menu at Pete's Tavern, around the corner from the Hotel Irving. A brass plaque, commemorating that event, is affixed to the outside wall near the entrance.

In 1950 my parents moved uptown. Three apartments and nine years later, they returned to Gramercy Park, renting an ideal two-story atelier at the National Arts Club, whose address is 15 Gramercy Park. It abuts the Players Club, then an all-male club for actors and writers, where my father often announced he was going after dinner. The Players Club, founded by Edwin Booth (brother of John Wilkes Booth), welcomed their first female member, Helen Hayes, in 1989. Helen was the wife of my father's best friend, Charles MacArthur.

My father claimed that he had no imagination. His stories were ones he had lived, partially lived or were told to him. He merely embroidered them.

Barbara Bemelmans, 2020